GO NICK JR. DIEGO GO!™

Diego's Birthday Surprise

by Lara Bergen

illustrated by Art Martin

Ready-to-Read

Simon Spotlight/Nick Jr.
New York   London   Toronto   Sydney

Based on the TV series *Go, Diego, Go!*™ as seen on Nick Jr.®

SIMON SPOTLIGHT
An imprint of Simon & Schuster Children's Publishing Division
1230 Avenue of the Americas, New York, New York 10020
Manufactured in the United States of America
First Edition
2 4 6 8 10 9 7 5 3 1
Library of Congress Cataloging-in-Publication Data
Bergen, Lara.
Diego's birthday surprise / by Lara Bergen ; illustrated by Art Mawhinney.
— 1st ed.
p. cm. — (Ready-to-read ; [level 1])
"Based on the TV series Go, Diego, Go! as seen on Nick Jr."
ISBN-13: 978-1-4169-5431-6
ISBN-10: 1-4169-5431-7
I. Mawhinney, Art. II. Go, Diego, go! (Television program) III. Title.
PZ7.B44985Dim 2008
2007027668

Hi! My name is  .
DIEGO

This is .
ALICIA

Do you know what today is?

It is  BABY JAGUAR 's birthday!

We will have a party.

It will be a surprise party!

ALICIA has a LIST of all of the

things we need.

First on the list is .

CHORIZO

 is a special treat

CHORIZO

for .

BABY JAGUAR

He loves to eat meat.

What else is on the  ?

We need party HATS , PRESENTS ,

and BALLOONS .

We have 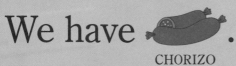.

CHORIZO

We have party snacks for everyone!

We have party .

HATS

We have  .

PRESENTS

But where are the  ?

BALLOONS

HAPP

Look out the  !

WINDOW

The  have the !

BOBOS

BALLOONS

Say "Freeze,  !"
BOBOS

Oops!

The  let the
BOBOS
go!
BALLOONS
They are sorry.

Hurry! We have to get the  BALLOONS back! BABY JAGUAR will be at the ANIMAL RESCUE CENTER soon!

 can help us find

the  .

Just say "  !"

 CLICK

RAINFOREST

will zoom through the

to look for the

BALLOONS

Are these  ?

No, those are .

Are these ?

The **BALLOONS** are up in the **TREE** .

RESCUE PACK can help us

get up the **TREE** to the **BALLOONS** .

Can we use a  to

KAYAK

reach the top of the 🌳 ?

TREE

No.

Can we climb a 🪜 to

LADDER

reach the top of the 🌳 ?

TREE

Yes!

Hooray!

We did it!

We got the 🎈 !

BALLOONS

Look! It is .

ALICIA

We need to hurry.

 is coming!

BABY JAGUAR

Let's go!
We have to get the  **BALLOONS**
back to the
ANIMAL RESCUE CENTER
fast.

Yeah!

We made it just in time.

Surprise!

Happy birthday,  !

BABY JAGUAR